One Little Balsam Fir

A Northwoods Counting Book

by Lesley A. DuTemple
Illustrated by Susan Robinson

©2006 Avery Color Studios, Inc.
ISBN-13: 978-1-892384-37-9, ISBN-10: 1-892384-37-X, Library of Congress Control Number: 2005935595
First Edition 2006, Published by Avery Color Studios, Inc. 511 D Avenue, Gwinn, MI 49841
Call 1-800-722-9925 for a catalog of other products.

1

One little balsam fir,
standing all alone.

2

Two great horned
owls came by to say hello.

3

Three loons came calling,
with their eyes all shiny red,

4

and **Four** little harebells
raised their purple heads.

5

Five golden buttercups
started dancing in the sun,

6

and **Six** herring gulls
stopped by to join the fun.

7

Seven Canada geese
came slowly drifting by,

8

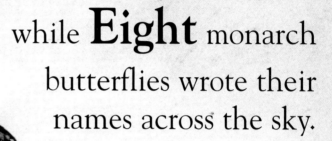

while **Eight** monarch
butterflies wrote their
names across the sky.

9

Nine shaggy moose
came marching in a row,

10

and **Ten** ox-eye daisies
sprang up to watch the show.

"Look!"

One little balsam fir
standing all alone?

Glossary

 **Balsam Fir** is the most symmetrical (evenly shaped) of all evergreens. A spicy fragrance is released when the needles or bark are crushed.

 **Great Horned Owls** are twice the size of crows that often harass them. Like all owls, their eyes are fixed in their sockets so they must turn their entire head to look at something.

 Common Loons live almost entirely on water, coming ashore only to breed and nest. Excellent divers, they actually swim underwater to catch food. Listen for their yodeling call.

 **Harebells** have a thin wiry stem with pointy bell-shaped flowers. Usually purple or blue, they can also be white or pink.

 Buttercups grow nearly 3 feet high and like wet meadows. Each flower has 5 to 7 glossy overlapping petals.

 **Herring Gulls** live near lakes and seashores. They have a loud bugle-like call and love to soar high overhead.

 **Canada Geese** breed and congregate along lakeshores. When migrating (traveling because of seasonal changes), they fly in a "V" or long line, and will travel both day and night.

 **Monarch Butterflies** migrate southward every fall. Birds avoid eating them because Monarchs eat milkweed, which gives them a bad taste.

 **Moose** are one of the largest members of the deer family, often weighing 1100 pounds. They eat aquatic plants (plants that grow in water) and other vegetation.

 Ox-Eye Daisies grow 3 feet high and like bright sunlight. They have white petals, notched at the tip, and a bright yellow center.

About The Author

Lesley A. DuTemple has written and published more than 20 children's books. The idea for One Little Balsam Fir came to her while hiking at Isle Royale National Park, carrying her daughter in a backpack. "It was raining, cold, and miserable. After stumbling one too many times, I started making up a rhyme to keep my hiking pace and take my mind off the water dripping down my neck." She lives in Michigan's Keweenaw Peninsula, on the shore of Lake Superior with her husband, two children, a very fluffy cat, and two huge dogs (who seem to always be covered in sand).

About The Artist

Susan Robinson is mostly a self-taught artist who has had a lifelong interest in art and the natural world. She divides her time creating paintings of minerals, pebbles, birds and other wildlife. The artist finds an abundance of inspiration and subject matter in the woods and along the beaches of the Keweenaw Peninsula of Michigan, where she lives with her husband.